Limer...

9112000017 0853

Also compiled by John Foster

101 Favourite Poems
A Century of Children's Poems
Ridiculous Rhymes
Dead Funny
Teasing Tongue-Twisters
Seriously Scary Poems
Completely Crazy Poems

Loopy Limericks

picked by John Foster

Illustrated by Julian Mosedale

belongs to
me

HarperCollins *Children's Books*

First published by Collins in 2001
Collins is an imprint of HarperCollins*Publishers* Ltd,
77-85 Fulham Palace Road, Hammersmith, W6 8JB

The HarperCollins *Children's Books* website address is:
www.harpercollinschildrensbooks.co.uk

This edition copyright © John Foster 2001
Illustrations by Julian Mosedale 2001
Back cover poem *Miss Nits* copyright © Andrea Shavick 2001
The acknowledgements on page 95-96 constitute
an extension of this copyright page.

ISBN 978-0-00-711181-7

The authors, illustrator and compiler assert the moral right to
be identified as the authors, illustrator and compiler of this work.

Conditions of Sale

Without limiting the rights under copyright reserved above,
this book is sold subject to the condition
that it shall not, by way of trade or otherwise,
be lent, re-sold, hired out or otherwise circulated
without both the publishers and copyright owner's
prior written consent in any form,
binding or cover other than that in which it is
published and without a similar condition
including this condition being imposed
on the subsequent purchaser.

BRENT LIBRARIES	
91120000170853	
Askews & Holts	10-Jan-2014
J821.08	£6.99

ANIMAL CRACKERS

A Wisp of a Wasp

I'm a wisp of a wasp with a worry,

I'm hiding somewhere in Surrey,

I've just bit upon

The fat sit upon

Of the King — so I left in a hurry!

Colin West

A Glow-worm Once Asked a Close Friend

A glow-worm once asked a close friend,

'Have you got a crash-helmet to lend?

There's a well-meaning lout

Who keeps stamping me out

In mistake for a cigarette-end!'

Noel Ford

A Yak From the Hills of Iraq

A yak from the hills of Iraq

Met a yak he had known awhile back.

They went out to dine

And talked of lang syne –

Yak-ety, yak-ety, yak.

Willard R. Espy

The Pelican

A rare old bird is the Pelican

His beak holds more than his belican.

　He can take in his beak

　Enough food for a week.

I'm darned if I know how the helican!

Dixon Merritt

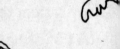

The Old Man of Tralee

There was an old man of Tralee,

who was horribly bored by a bee.

When they asked, 'Does it buzz?'

He replied, 'Yes, it does,

It's a regular brute of a bee.'

Edward Lear

Duck Down

A duck that's known as an Eider

Has down all over outside'er

I know it's absurd

But cook ate the whole bird

Now she has eiderdown duck down inside'er.

David Whitehead

The Young Lady of Riga

There was a young lady of Riga

Who went for a ride on a tiger:

    They returned from the ride

    With the lady inside

And a smile on the face of the tiger.

Anon

High-level Gorilla

A large and hairy gorilla
Finding a fat caterpillar.
Said, 'I simply abhor
Eating anything raw,
Shall I boil'er, or fry'er or grill'er?'

David Whitehead

A Hungry Old Goat Called Heather

A hungry old goat called Heather,
~~Was tied up with an old bit of leather.~~
In a minute or two
She had chewed it right through,
And that was the end of her tether.

Celia McMaster

An Elephant Born in Tibet

An elephant born in Tibet
One day in its cage wouldn't get.
 So its keeper stood near –
 Stuck a hose in its ear.
And invented the first Jumbo Jet.

Anon

A TV-Mad Tortoise Named Trish

A TV-mad tortoise named Trish

For a satellite telly did wish,

So she stripped off – it's true!

And proceeded to view

With her shell as the aerial dish.

Noel Ford

Chutney

A gastronomical cat from Putney

Concocted a wonderful chutney

Bits of old lamb

Mixed with strawberry jam

Which tasted sweet and yet muttony.

Roger McGough

Down Under

A most considerate bird is the Kiwi,

It roosts at the top of a pea-tree.

It goes to the loo

In everyones' view.

Shouting 'Look out! Here comes the wee-wee'.

David Whitehead

A Poem to Emus

The problem with keeping some emus

Is telling which ones are the she'mus.

They all have long legs,

But, only one lays the eggs.

Those that don't are obviously the he'mus.

David Whitehead

Dotty Dressers

The Young Lady of Wilts

There was a young lady of Wilts

Who walked up to Scotland on stilts;

When they said it was shocking

To show so much stocking,

She answered, 'Then what about kilts?'

Edward Lear

The Young Man of Bengal

There was a young man of Bengal
Who went to a fancy-dress ball,
    He went, just for fun,
    Dressed up as a bun,
And a dog ate him up in the hall.

Anon

Twickenham Twit

A rugby star playing at Twickenham
Wore shorts far too tight to run quick in 'em
They pinched round the waist
Were not in good taste
And quite frankly he looked a right twit in 'em.

Richard Caley

There Was a Hell's Angel From Bude

There was a Hell's Angel from Bude

Whose skin was completely tattooed

From his head to his toe

So no one would know

That he rode his bike in the nude.

Paul Cookson

A Thrifty Young Fellow of Shoreham

A thrifty young fellow of Shoreham
Made brown paper trousers and woreham;
    He looked nice and neat
    Till he bent in the street
To pick up a pin; then he toreham.

Anon

Sir Bert

There once was a knight, called Sir Bert,
Who said, 'Oh, this armour does hurt!
    I can stand it no more;
    Nip down to the store
And fetch me a non-iron shirt.'

Gerard Benson

The Fella From Reading

There was this young fella from Reading

Who got lost in a mountain of bedding

They found his pyjamas

In the Bahamas

Being worn by a bride at her wedding!

Ernest Henry

When She Bought Some Pyjamas in Cheltenham

When she bought some pyjamas in Cheltenham
A lady was asked how she felt in 'em.
 She said, 'Winter's all right,
 But on a hot night
I'm afraid that I'm going to melt in 'em.'

Anon

Trendy Wendy

There once was a young girl called Wendy
Who liked to wear clothes that were trendy
She wore platform heels
And you know how that feels
It made both her ankles go bendy.

Brenda Williams

A Vain Polar Bear

A vain polar bear, name of Lily,

Liked clothes that were flimsy and frilly,

She swapped her thick fleece

For a lacy two-piece,

So she's chic but exceedingly chilly.

Julia Rawlinson

A Dancing Black Bear

There once was a dancing black bear,

Who, instead of a hat, wore a pair

  Of boots on his head.

  'It's the two-step', he said,

'And it feels like walking on air!'

J. Patrick Lewis

Dreadful Disasters

There Was an Old Man of Blackheath

There was an old man of Blackheath

Who sat on his set of false teeth.

Said he with a start,

'Oh Lord bless my heart!

I have bitten myself underneath!'

Anon

There Was a Young Lady Named Rose

There was a young lady named Rose

Who had a huge wart on her nose

When she had it removed

Her appearance improved

But her glasses slipped down to her toes.

Anon

A Surgeon From Glasgow Named Mac

A surgeon from Glasgow named Mac,

Once forgot to put everything back.

As his train made to start,

His case came apart,

And a kidney rolled down off the rack.

Michael Palin

The Canoe-Builder

There was a young man from Crewe,

Who wanted to build a canoe;

    He went to the river

    And found with a shiver

He hadn't used waterproof glue.

Lorna Bain

A Painter Who Lived in West Ditting

A painter who lived in West Ditting

Interrupted two girls with their knitting.

He said with a sigh,

'That park bench – well I

Just painted it, right where you're sitting.'

Anon

Oops!

There once was an elegant Miss

Who said, 'I think skating is bliss.'

    This no more will she state,

    For a wheel off her skate

Made her end up something like this.

Anon

Silly Races

There was a young man of Belfast,

Who ran in a race and came last;

He said: 'That's enough!

I'm all out of puff,'

As a tortoise came thundering past.

Carol Stevenson

A Split Personality

A gymnastic young Miss from St Kitts
liked to show off her skill at the splits,
but she took it too far
on the parallel bar
and got split into two equal bits.

Colin Macfarlane

There Was a Young Fellow Named Tom

There was a young fellow named Tom
Who invented a large home-made bomb.
    If you need dynamite
    Consult his website:
Blowupandtakecover.com

Pam Gidney

How Awkward When Playing With Glue

How awkward when playing with glue

To suddenly find out that you

Have stuck nice and tight

Your left hand to your right

In a permanent how-do-you-do?

Constance Levy

A Young Joker Named Tarr

There was a young joker named Tarr
Who playfully pickled his Ma.
    When he finished his work
    He remarked with a smirk,
'This will make quite a family jar.'

Anon

A Young Fellow Called Mark

There was a young fellow called Mark
Who would swim out to sea in the dark.
On these night-time trips
He saw lots of ships
Until he was seen by a shark.

Anon

Not Such a High Flyer

There was an old man who averred

He had learned how to fly like a bird.

  Cheered by thousands of people

  He leapt from the steeple –

This tomb states the date it occurred.

Anon

A Daring Young Acrobat

A daring young acrobat, Fritz,

did as his finale the splits.

It raised a big laugh

when he split right in half

and was carried away in two bits.

Marian Swinger

Ghostly Groans

There Once Was a Pale Apparition

There once was a pale apparition

Who suffered from grave malnutrition.

Said Mom, 'You'll be a ghost,

If you don't eat your toast.'

Answered he, 'That's just superstition.'

Ann McGovern

Promotion

A keen traffic warden named Hector
Was killed by a hit-and-run rector.
    With evident pride
    Hector sighed as he died
'This makes me a traffic in-SPECTRE.'

Ian Serraillier

A Skeleton Once in Khartoum

A skeleton once in Khartoum
Invited a ghost to his room;
    They spent the whole night
    In the eeriest fright
As to which should be frightened of whom.

Anon

All Aboard

'He's rung his last bell,' mourners cried,
When their bus-conductor friend died,
Then the coffin-lid groaned,
And a voice inside moaned:
'There's room for two standing inside!'

Willis Hall

A Phantom called Pete

There once was a phantom called Pete,
Who never would play, drink or eat.
He said, 'I don't care
For a Coke or éclair –
Can't you see that I'm dead on my feet?'

Anon

A Skeleton, Fatty O'Hyatt

A Skeleton, Fatty O'Hyatt,

Went on a low-calorie diet.

Although he got little,

His bones were so brittle

He snapped. He was silly to try it.

Kaye Umansky

A Foolish Young Girl

A foolish young girl called Sheree
went and stood under a tree,
but thunder was crashing
and lightning was flashing.
'Oops!' said her ghost, 'Silly me.'

Marian Swinger

A Ghost Called Paul

There once was a ghost called Paul,
Who went to a fancy-dress ball.
  To shock all the guests
  He went quite undressed
But the rest couldn't see him at all.

Anon

Musical Madness

A Tutor Who Tooted the Flute

A tutor who tooted the flute
Tried to tutor two tooters to toot.
   Said the two to the tutor,
    'Is it harder to toot or
To tutor two tooters to toot?'

Carolyn Wells

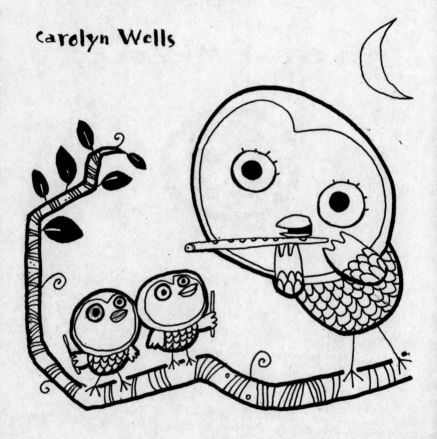

There Was a Pop Singer Called Fred

There was a pop singer called Fred

Who sang through the top of his head.

It came as a blow

When the notes were too low

So he sang through his toenails instead.

Max Fatchen

There Was a Young Teacher Called Phinn

There was a young teacher called Phinn

Whose legs were incredibly thin

When he did the high kicks

They resembled drum sticks

And he played the 'Top Ten' on his chin.

Lesley Calder

The Music Examiner

The music examiner stood
As I played as well as I could
But, shaking his head
'An oboe,' he said
'Is an ill-wind that no one blows good.'

Philip C. Gross

A Silly Young Goblin Named Crumpet

A silly young goblin named Crumpet
Decided he'd like to play trumpet.
A trumpet, you know,
Works fine if you blow,
But not, if like Crumpet, you thump it.

Kaye Umansky

A Young Girl in the Choir

There was a young girl in the choir
Whose voice arose higher and higher,
Till one Sunday night
It rose quite out of sight
And they found it next day on the spire.

Anon

45

An Opera Star Named Maria

An opera star named Maria
Always tried to sing higher and higher,
Till she hit a high note
Which got stuck in her throat –
Then she entered the heavenly Choir.

Anon

Heartbeat Chartbeat

There once were five patients from Barts
With irregular beats to their hearts;
They recorded the sound
And, with pleasure, they found
That they reached Number One in the Charts!

Trevor Harvey

Monstrous Moments

The Monster's Lament

Cried Frankenstein's Monster: 'By heck!

I feel like a physical wreck!

My face has more stitches,

Than two pairs of britches,

And these bolts are a pain in the neck!'

Willis Hall

An Adventurous Lady Called Florrie

An adventurous lady called Florrie

Had a monster she kept in a quarry.

But it didn't like plants

And ate both of her aunts

Although later it said it was sorry.

Nick Timms

A Monstrous Problem

Said the monster deep down in Loch Ness,

'How I long for a change of address,

Without this pollution,

And constant confusion,

From the tourists who make such a mess!'

Willis Hall

The Sea-Serpent

A sea-serpent saw a big tanker,

Bit a hole in her side and then sank her.

    It swallowed the crew

    In a minute or two

And then picked its teeth with the anchor.

Anon

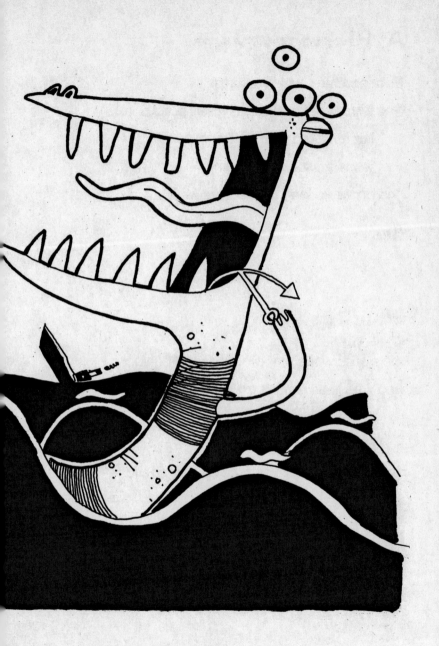

A Plesiosaurus

There once was a plesiosaurus
Who lived when the world was all porous.
>   But it fainted with shame
>   When it first heard its name
And departed long ages before us.

Anon

Hannibal

There once was a schoolboy named Hannibal
Who won local fame as a cannibal
>   By eating his mother,
>   His father, his brother,
And his two sisters, Gertrude and Annabelle.

Anon

Potty People

Take the Curious Case of Tom Pettigrew

Take the curious case of Tom Pettigrew
And Hetty, his sister. When Hettigrew
    As tall as a tree
    She came just to Tom's knee.
And did **Tom** keep on growing? You bettigrew.

David McCord

My Sister

My sister's remarkably light,
She can float to a fabulous height.
It's a troublesome thing,
But we tie her with string,
And we use her instead of a kite.

Margaret Mahy

A Young Girl From Gloucester

There was a young girl from Gloucester,

Whose parents thought they had lost her.

From the fridge came a sound

And at last she was found.

The trouble was – how to defrost her?

Anon

An Odd Fellow From Tyre

There was an odd fellow from Tyre

Who constantly sat on the fire.

When asked, 'Are you hot?'

He said, 'Certainly not,

I'm James Winterbottom, Esquire.'

Anon

The Young Lady of Tottenham

There was a young lady of Tottenham,

Who'd no manners, or else she'd forgotten 'em.

At tea at the vicar's

She tore off her knickers

Because, she explained, she felt 'ot in 'em.

Anon

An Old Man of Darjeeling

There was an old man of Darjeeling

Who travelled from London to Ealing.

It said on the door

'Please don't spit on the floor,'

So he carefully spat on the ceiling.

Anon

A Young Woman Named Dotty

There was a young woman named Dotty

Who said as she sat on her potty,

'It isn't polite

To do this in sight,

But then who am I to be snotty?'

Anon

Strange Tastes

A bad-mannered man named McDade
Ate breakfast with a rake, hoe and spade.
While wearing his slippers
He liked to eat kippers
And sausage with sweet marmalade.

Marguerite Varday

Ridiculous Romances

She Frowned and Called Him Mr

She frowned and called him Mr.

Because in sport he kr.

> And so, in spite

> That very night

This Mr. Kr. Sr.

Anon

A Ghoul and His Girl For a Lark

A ghoul and his girl, for a lark,

Went strolling one night in the park.

> They stopped under a light

> And the ghoul cried in fright

EEK! Quick, dear, get back in the dark!

Ann McGovern

The Old Maiden From Fife

There was an old maiden from Fife,

Who had never been kissed in her life;

Along came a cat,

And she said, 'I'll kiss that!'

But the cat answered, 'Not on your life!'

Anon

There's a Beautiful Girl in the Skies

There's a beautiful girl in the skies
Of an astronomical size.
   I gaze through my 'scope
    Each night in the hope
Of seeing the stars in her eyes.

Willard R. Espy

A Young Lady Called Millicent

There was a young lady called Millicent
Who hated the perfume that Willie sent,
    So she sent it to Liz
    Who declared, 'What a swizz
It's that silly scent Willie sent Millicent!'

Anon

A Dentist Named Archibald Moss

A dentist named Archibald Moss
Fell in love with the dainty Miss Ross,
Since he held in abhorrence
Her Christian name Florence,
He renamed her his dear dental Floss.

Anon

A Gardening Nut From O'Hare

A gardening nut from O'Hare

Grew apples and grapes in his hair.

    One day on the beach

    He met a young peach –

Now the peach and the nut are a pear.

Anon

The Skiing Expert

A lady, an expert on skis,

Went out with a man who said, 'Please,

On the next precipice

Will you give me a kiss?'

She said, 'Quick, before somebody sees!'

Anon

A High That Was Learning to Low

A High that was learning to Low
Met a Stop that was learning to Go.
>   They walked hand in hand
>   Till they came to a land
Of a Yes that was learning to No.

Willard R. Espy

Love At First Bite

A young cannibal known as Demeter
saw a young lady and wanted to meet her;
when they first got together
he could not decide whether
it was politer to kiss her or eat her!

Colin Macfarlane

School Sillies

A Chemistry Student From Gillingham

A chemistry student from Gillingham

Kept emptying jam jars and filling 'em

With a poisonous jelly

That was bright green and smelly

So he used it on teachers for killing 'em.

John Rice

A Young Lady From Slough

There was a young lady from Slough
Who went into school with her cow.
The cow was so bright
It got all its sums right
And it's two books ahead of her now.

Nick Timms

A Young Teacher From Staines

There was a young teacher from Staines
Who simply hated the use of Canes;
    He had other controls
    For deviant souls,
Such as plugging them into the Mains.

David R. Morgan

How to Deflate a Queen Bee

'I'm the bee's knees,' said posh Abigail.

'I'm top of the class, off the scale.'

Said Jack as she sat

On a hidden tin-tack,

'And now you've a sting in your tail!'

Patricia Leighton

A Heartless Young Fellow From Tweed

A heartless young fellow from Tweed

Took his dragon to school on a lead.

When he left it outside

It just sat there and cried

'Cause it wanted to learn how to read.

Nick Timms

A Bully Called Ray

Our school has a bully called Ray
Who copies my homework each day.
So last night out of spite
I did none of it right
Just my luck, 'cause today he's away.

Nick Timms

Get It Write!

There was wunce a yung skoolgirl from Welling
at hoom teechers were knostantly yeling
all her trubbles eggsisted
from the facked she rezisted
their atempts to encurrage gude speling!

Colin Macfarlane

In Summer

In summer at break we play cricket

But I really don't think I can stick it

For they roll up my pants

And make me take stance

And they use my thin legs as a wicket.

Philip C. Gross

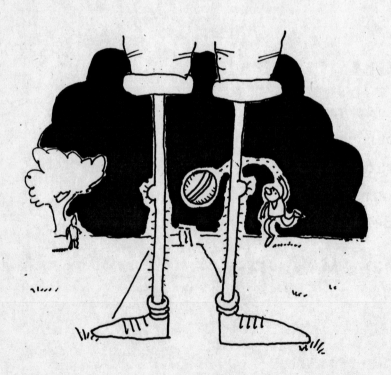

72

A Right-Handed Fellow Named Wright

A right-handed fellow named Wright,
In writing 'write' always wrote 'right.'
> Where he meant to write right,
> If he'd written 'write' right,
Wright would not have wrought rot writing 'rite.'

Anon

Said a Boy to his Teacher One Day

Said a boy to his teacher one day,
'Wright has not written 'rite' right, I say.'
> And the teacher replied,
> As the error she eyed,
'Right! Wright write 'write' right, right away.'

Anon

Miss Nits

My teacher is not very nice
Her hair is infested with lice
When my mother complained
The headmaster explained
She was all he could get for the price.

Andrea Shavick

Short Visit, Long Stay

Our school trip was a special occasion
But we never reached our destination
Instead of the zoo
I was locked in the loo
Of an M62 service station.

Paul Cookson

Traveller's Tales

There Was a Young Creature From Space

There was a young creature from space

Whose legs grew out of its face

The smell of its toes

Was so near its nose

It wore a clothes-peg just in case.

Steve Turner

A Skinny Old Fellow Called Prune

A skinny old fellow called Prune
took off in a massive balloon
but discovered, too late,
he was too light a weight
and soared all the way to the moon.

Marian Swinger

Problem Solved

As on Red Planet, Mars, we alighted,
A very large banner we sighted.
'That's the answer,' I said,
'To why Mars is called "red"'
It said MARTIANS ALL LOVE MAN UNITED.

Eric Finney

Relativity

There was a young lady named Bright,

Who travelled much faster than light,

    She started one day

    In the relative way,

And returned on the previous night.

Anon

The Young Lady From Crewe

There was a young lady from Crewe
Who wanted to catch the 2.02.
    Said a porter, 'Don't worry,
    Or hurry, or scurry,
It's a minute or two to 2.02.'

Anon

A Young Lady From Spain

There was a young lady from Spain
Who was dreadfully sick on a train,
Not once – but again,
and again and again
and again and again and again.

Anon

Back to Square One

An explorer who lived in Iran
thought he'd travel the world in a van.
But he bought an old hearse
that got stuck in reverse
and he ended up where he began!

Colin Macfarlane

Tummy Troubles

There Was a Young Man Called Strathspey

There was a young man called Strathspey

Who swallowed a pigeon one day.

He felt such a twerp

He made himself burp

And the pigeon flew out and away.

Michael Palin

An Amazing Fast Runner Called Murray

An amazing fast runner called Murray

Was always in a great hurry,

The reason they say

Was the trip to Bombay

Where he sampled a Vindaloo curry.

Andrew Henderson

An Explorer Named Mortimer Craft

An explorer named Mortimer Craft,

While in Africa ate spiced giraffe.

The effect of this food

Was a sound deep and rude

And green flames that shot out fore and aft.

Mick Gower

The Old Lady of Ryde

There was an old lady of Ryde
Who ate some green apples and died.
    The apples fermented
    Within the lamented
Making cider inside 'er inside.

Anon

I Sat Next to the Duchess at Tea

I sat next to the duchess at tea.
It was just as I feared it would be.
Her rumblings abdominal
Were simply phenomenal
And everyone thought it was me!

Anon

There Was an Old Man of Peru

There was an old man of Peru

Who dreamt he was eating his shoe.

    He woke in the night

    In a terrible fright

And found it was perfectly true.

Anon

Nelly Ninnis

There was a young girl called Nelly

Who had a nylon belly

The skin was so thin

We could all see in

It was full of Custard and Jelly.

Spike Milligan

Lew

I don't wish to harp about Lew
Who kept peering into the stew.
    He lifted the lid
    And in it he slid.
I think I'll miss dinner, don't you?

Max Fatchen

A Greedy Young Scrumper Called Sue

A greedy young scrumper called Sue
scoffed apples, pears, greengages too.
She consumed every core,
Then scrumped a few more
and spent all the next day on the loo.

Marian Swinger

A Young Lady From Ickenham

There was a young lady from Ickenham

Who went on a bus-trip to Twickenham.

She drank too much beer,

Which made her feel queer,

So she took off her boots and was sick-in-em.

Anon

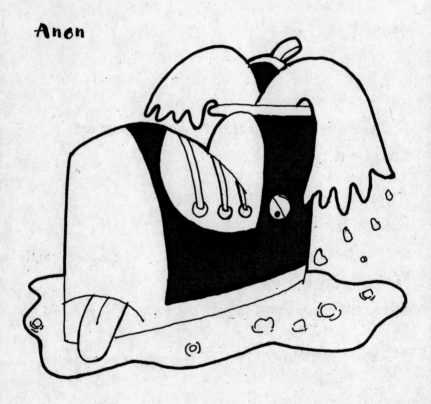

Vampire Bites

Vampoor

A vampire who didn't like gore
Cut his fingers and let out a roar.
His friends rallied round
As he sat on the ground
Each armed with a glass and a straw.

Sally Farrell Odgers

The Biter Bit

A vampire out on the spree,
Got what he deserved, believe me,
When he went through a night,
Without getting a bite,
But got bitten himself by a flea.

Willis Hall

A Werewolf Named Wendy

A werewolf named Wendy is fair,
So long as the sun is up there.
　　But when the moon rises,
　　She puts on disguises –
With fangs and a lot of coarse hair.

Ann McGovern

A Foolish Young Dentist Called Keith

A foolish young dentist called Keith

Agreed to clean Dracula's teeth,

No more is he drilling.

Instead he is filling

A whopping great hole on the heath.

Kaye Umansky

Last Writes

A Last Word

To those readers I've sent round the bend

I should mention I didn't intend

to drive anyone mad

but at least you'll be glad

you're at last at the part marked:

THE END!

Colin Macfarlane

Acknowledgements

We are grateful to the following authors for permission to include the following poems, all of which are published for the first time in this collection:

Gerard Benson: 'Sir Bert' copyright © Gerard Benson 2001. Richard Caley: 'Twickenham Twit' copyright © Richard Caley 2001. Paul Cookson: 'There Was a Hell's Angel From Bude' and 'Short Visit, Long Stay' both copyright © Paul Cookson 2001. Eric Finney: 'Problem Solved' copyright © Eric Finney 2001. Pam Gidney: 'There Was a Young Fellow Named Tom' copyright © Pam Gidney 2001. Trevor Harvey: 'Heartbeat, Chartbeat' copyright © Trevor Harvey 2001. Patricia Leighton: 'How to Deflate a Queen Bee' copyright © Patricia Leighton 2001. J. Patrick Lewis: 'A Dancing Black Bear' copyright © J. Patrick Lewis 2001. Colin Macfarlane: 'A Split Personality', 'Love At First Bite', 'Get It Write!', 'Back To Square One' and 'A Last Word' all copyright © Colin Macfarlane 2001. Andrea Shavick: 'Miss Nits' copyright © Andrea Shavick 2001. Julia Rawlinson: 'A Vain Polar Bear' copyright © Julia Rawlinson 2001. Marian Swinger: 'A Skinny Old Fellow Called Prune', 'A Greedy Young Scrumper Called Sue', 'A Daring Young Acrobat' and 'A Foolish Young Girl' all copyright © Marian Swinger 2001. David Whitehead: 'Duck Down', 'High-level Gorilla', 'A Poem to Emus' and 'Down Under' all copyright © David Whitehead 2001. Brenda Williams: 'Trendy Wendy' copyright © Brenda Williams 2001.

We also acknowledge permission to include previously published poems:

Willard R. Espy: 'A Yak from the Hills of Iraq', 'There's a Beautiful Girl in the Skies' and 'A High That Was Learning To Low' from *A Children's Alamanac of Words At Play* by Willard R.Espy copyright © 1982 by Willard R. Espy. Used by permission of Clarkson Potter/Publishers, a division of Random House, Inc. Max Fatchen: 'There Was a Pop Singer Called Fred' and 'Lew' from *Songs For My Dog and Other People* (Kestrel 1980), included by permission of John Johnson (Authors' Agent) Ltd. Mick Gowar: 'An Explorer Called Mortimer Craft' copyright © 1984 Mick Gowar included by permission of the author. Philip C. Gross: 'The Music Examiner', 'In Summer' copyright © 1988 Philip C. Gross first published in *School's Out* (Oxford University Press), included by permission of the author. Noel Ford: 'A Glow-Worm Once Asked a Close Friend' (p.7), and 'A TV-Mad Tortoise Named Trish' (p.14) from *Limeroons* by Noel Ford (Puffin 1991) copyright © Noel Ford 1991. Reproduced by permission of Penguin Books Ltd. Willis Hall: 'All Aboard', 'The Monster's Lament', 'A Monstrous Problem' and 'The Biter Bit' from *Spooky Rhymes* copyright © Willis Hall. First published by Hamlyn Publishing Group Ltd, now

Egmont Children's Books Limited and used with permission. Ernest Henry: 'The Fella From Reading' from *Not More Poems To Shout Out Loud*. Used by permission of Bloomsbury Publishing Plc. Constance Levy: 'How Awkward While Playing With Glue' from *I'm Going To Pet a Worm Today and Other Poems* by Constance Levy (McElderry Books). Copyright © 1991 by Constance Kling Levy. Used by permission of Marian Reiner for the author. Roger McGough: 'Chutney' from *Bad Bad Cats* (Viking 1997) copyright © Roger McGough 1997. Reprinted by permission of PFD on behalf of Roger McGough. Margaret Mahy 'My Sister' from *Nonstop Nonsense* by Margaret Mahy (J.M.Dent and Sons). Reprinted by permission of The Orion Publishing Group Ltd. Spike Milligan: 'Nelly Ninnis' copyright © 1981 Spike Milligan Productions Ltd from *Unspun Socks From a Chicken's Laundry* (M & J Hobbs) used by permission of Spike Milligan Productions Ltd. David R. Morgan: 'A Young Teacher From Staines' copyright © 1988 David R. Morgan, first published in *School's Out* edited by John Foster (Oxford University Press), included by permission of the author. Sally Farrell Odgers: 'Vampoor' from *Putrid Poems* Omnibus included by permission of the author. Michael Palin: 'A Surgeon From Glasgow Named Mac' and 'There Was a Young Man Called Strathspey' from *Limericks* by Michael Palin, published by Hutchinson/Red Fox. Used by permission of The Random House Group Limited. John Rice: 'A Chemistry Student From Gillingham' copyright © 1988 John Rice. First published in *School's Out* edited by John Foster (Oxford University Press), included by permission of the author. Ian Serraillier: 'Promotion' copyright © 1990 Ian Serraillier, used by permission of Anne Serraillier. Nick Timms: 'An Adventurous Lady Called Florrie', 'A Young Lady From Slough', 'A Bully Called Ray' and 'A Heartless Young Fellow From Tweed' copyright © 2001 Nick Timms included by permission of the author. Steve Turner: 'There Was a Young Creature From Space' copyright © 1999 Steve Turner from *Dad You're Not Funny* (Lion). Used by permission of Lion Publishing PLC. Kaye Umansky: 'A Skeleton Fatty O'Hyatt', 'A Silly Young Goblin Named Crumpet' and 'A Foolish Young Dentist Called Keith' copyright © 1988 Kaye Umansky, included by permission of the author. Marguerite Varday: 'Strange Tastes' included by permission of the author. Colin West: 'A Wisp of a Wasp' from *The Best of West* (Hutchinson) copyright © 1990 Colin West, included by permission of the author.

Despite every effort to trace and contact copyright holders, this has not been possible in a few cases. If notified, the publisher will be pleased to rectify any errors or omissions at the earliest opportunity.

Printed by RR Donnelley at Glasgow, UK